ZOOM! ZOOM! ZOOM! I'm Off to the Moon!

dan yaccarino

SCHOLASTIC INC.

New York   Toronto   London   Auckland   Sydney
Mexico City   New Delhi   Hong Kong   Buenos Aires

Zoom! Zoom! Zoom! I'm off to the moon.

ISBN 0-439-36541-4

Copyright © 1997 by Dan Yaccarino
Published by Scholastic Inc.
SCHOLASTIC and associated logos are trademarks and/or registered trademarks of Scholastic Inc.

12 11 10 9 8 7 6 5 4 3 2 1   3 4 5 6 7/0

Printed in the U.S.A.   08

First Scholastic trade printing, January 2002

The illustrations are alkyds on watercolor paper. The type was set in Bernhard Gothic Ultra. Design by Kristina Iulo.

Up, up, and away,
I'm leaving today.

First, space suit,

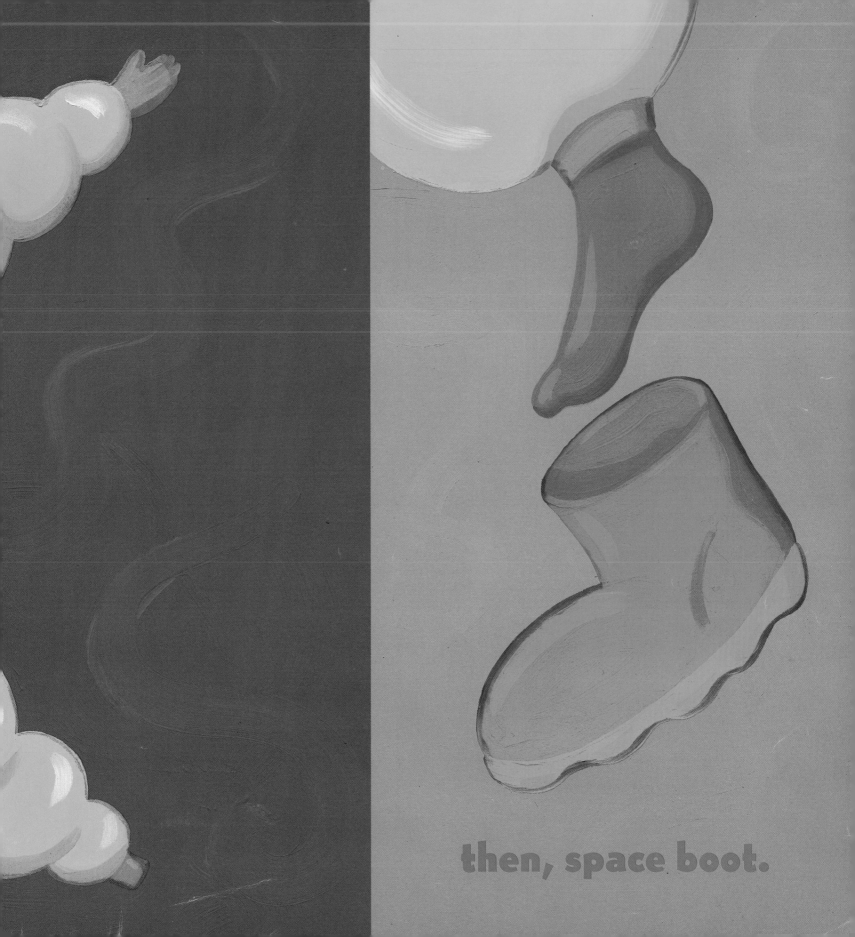

then, space boot.

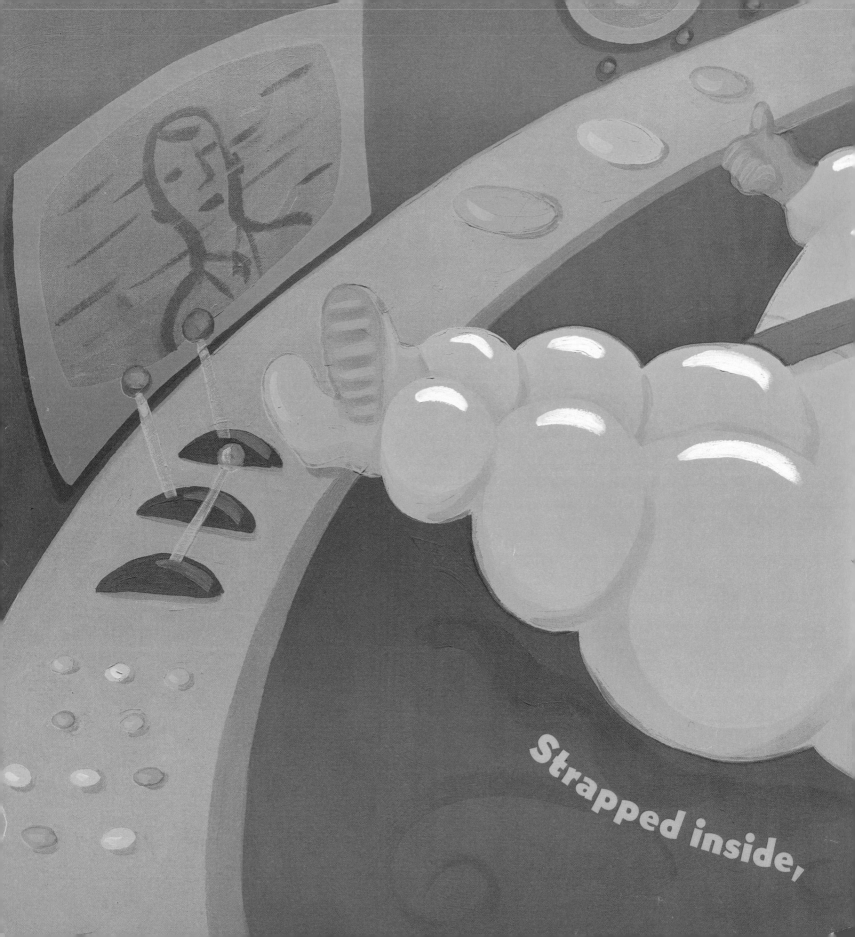

Strapped inside,

I'm ready to ride!

0 1. 2

Countdown counting...
Excitement mounting...

Boosters blast!

Moving fast.

Engines roaring.

Rocket soaring.

First stage, engines fire.

Second stage, flying higher.

Third stage, engines tire.

There's outer space all over the place.

Floating around without a sound.

Just avoid the asteroids.

Dark skies.

Earthrise.

See you later,
lunar crater.

Comets fly.
Now say...

...Good-bye.

LIGHTS WINKING.

PANELS

BLINKING.

BUTTONS
AND
DIALS

COUNT THE MILES.

A sonic boom. I'm landing soon.

Across the nation —

CeLeBraTIoN!

...from the moon.